# Five reasons why you'll love Mirabelle...

Mirabelle is magical and mischievous!

Mirabelle is half witch, half fairy, and totally naughty!

She loves making potions with her travelling potion kit!

Mirabelle loves sprinkling a sparkle of mischief wherever she goes!

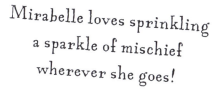

She has a little baby dragon called Violet!

# What would you like to do at a witchy sleepover?

Dress up in lots of different
witches' hats!
– Jojo

Mix a special potion that
makes everyone giggle
uncontrollably.
– Meghan

Tell a-little-bit scary
ghost stories with a torch
in a pillow fort.
– Skyler

Have broomstick races
around the bedroom.
– Melody

Cast spells to make toys come to
life and play with them.
– Polly

Look outside for magical
ingredients for our potions!
– Darcy

# Family Tree

My Mum
Seraphina Starspell

My brother
Wilbur Starspell

My Dad
Alvin Starspell

Me!
Mirabelle Starspell

Violet

Illustrated by Mike Love, based on
original artwork by Harriet Muncaster

## OXFORD
### UNIVERSITY PRESS

Great Clarendon Street, Oxford OX2 6DP
Oxford University Press is a department of the University of Oxford.
It furthers the University's objective of excellence in research, scholarship,
and education by publishing worldwide. Oxford is a registered trade mark
of Oxford University Press in the UK and in certain other countries

Database right Oxford University Press (maker)

First published in 2024

British Library Cataloguing in Publication Data

Data available

ISBN: 978-0-19-278378-3

1 3 5 7 9 10 8 6 4 2

Printed in China

Paper used in the production of this book is a natural,
recyclable product made from wood grown in sustainable forests.
The manufacturing process conforms to the environmental
regulations of the country of origin.

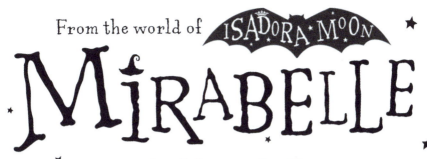

From the world of ISADORA MOON

# MIRABELLE

## and the Midnight Feast

# Harriet Muncaster

OXFORD
UNIVERSITY PRESS

Ameera-Rose,
Happy Reading!
with love, magic *
and sparkle.* * .

Harriet Muncaster

X

# Chapter ONE

It was almost the end of the school day, and I was finding it *very* hard to concentrate in spellcasting class.

'Mirabelle!' came Miss Spindlewick's voice through my daydreams. 'Sit up and listen and control that dragon!'

I immediately sat up straight and looked for my little pet dragon Violet.

I couldn't afford to get into trouble today.
I was supposed to be going straight
home with my best friend Carlotta that
afternoon for a sleepover! I was so excited,
I couldn't *wait*. If Miss Spindlewick put
me in after-school detention, that would
ruin everything! I found Violet down
at my feet, blowing purple flames and
scorching the floor, so I quickly lifted her
onto my lap and hoped Miss Spindlewick
wouldn't notice the marks.

Finally, *finally*, the bell rang for the end of school, and I gathered up all my books, shoving them into my satchel. Violet fluttered excitedly next to my ear.

'Yay!' said Carlotta. 'Home time at last! I can't wait for our sleepover, Mirabelle. Mum's even got some fairy food in for you to eat. I know you hate witch food. I think we should stay up really late and have a *midnight feast*!'

'Definitely!' I said.

We collected our capes and brooms and walked out into the playground to wait for Carlotta's big sister Edith. We soon saw her sauntering out of the school, her hair twirled up into two cool space buns. She pretended not to see us and just hopped onto her broomstick and rose into the air. We followed her, chattering excitedly.

Carlotta lives on the other side of town from me, near the forest of tall, dark fir trees. As we flew towards her house, a delicious shiver rippled through me from the top of my head to the tips of my toes. It feels a lot witchier where Carlotta lives! I love going there. It's fun getting to pretend I'm full witch for a while. My dad is a fairy and my mum is a witch, which makes me a bit of both, but I *definitely* enjoy my witch side more!

Edith swooped down towards a black house with a spiky roof and a front door the colour of elderberries. It immediately flew open, and Carlotta's mum stood there.

'Witchlings!' she cried. 'How was your day at school? Hello Mirabelle, it's nice to see you!'

I beamed at Mrs Cobweb as I skidded down onto the front path and slipped my suitcase off my broomstick. I followed Carlotta inside to the kitchen where Edith

was already rummaging in the cupboards
for a packet of squashed-fly biscuits.

'Oh, don't take them all, Edith!' cried
Carlotta, running over to her big sister. But
Edith swooped the biscuits out of Carlotta's
reach and disappeared with them.

'Humph,' said Carlotta, before sniffing the air. 'What's that smell?'

'I've made cupcakes!' said Mrs Cobweb. 'In honour of Mirabelle's visit, I used a fairy recipe as I know she doesn't like witch food. It used some very strange ingredients . . . Flour, sugar, butter, and *blossom petals*!'

She took a tray of cakes out of the oven and placed them onto a cooling rack. Carlotta wrinkled her nose.

'They look very *sweet*,' Carlotta said.

'I thought so too,' said Mrs Cobweb, 'which is why I made an extra tray of spider-leg witch cakes for us! They need to stay in the oven for a bit longer to char.'

'Oh yum!' said Carlotta. 'My favourite! Thanks, Mum!'

I took one of the fairy cakes and followed Carlotta out to the garden while we waited for the witch cakes. I love going into Carlotta's garden. It's full of all kinds of magical plants perfect for spells and potions. It is witchy and wild, with big, spotted, poisonous toadstools that glow in the dark, clumps of fierce stinging nettles that you have to hop over carefully, and spiky, twisting, thorny brambles sprouting velvety roses. There's even a big cauldron hot tub on the patio by the back door!

'We can go in it if you like?' said Carlotta. 'You can borrow a swimsuit!'

'Sure!' I replied.

Carlotta and I ran back into the house to change. On the way out, Carlotta grabbed a charcoal-blackened spider-leg witch cake, and we leapt into the hot tub together.

'Ooh, it's boiling!' I said, feeling my cheeks turn red.

'You get used to it,' said Carlotta, unperturbed.

Sometimes I wonder if full witches have thicker skin!

We stayed in the hot tub for a while, chatting and laughing. Purple bubbles foamed all around us and green steam hissed into the air.

'By the way,' Carlotta said, 'I did promise Mum and Dad that we wouldn't use any magic tonight.'

'That's OK!' I replied. I felt so happy in that moment that I wasn't even *thinking* about magic! My fingers itch for spellcasting sometimes if I'm feeling a bit bored, but I'm never bored at Carlotta's house. There are always so many things to do!

'*Edith's* allowed to use magic whenever she wants!' said Carlotta resentfully.

'I suppose she *is* older,' I replied. 'And she doesn't get into as much mischief!'

'That's true,' sighed Carlotta. 'But you know what, Mirabelle? She's got this amazing new potion kit, all shiny and sleek, that Mum and Dad bought her recently. They didn't buy *me* a new potion kit!'

I sat up with a splash, my interest piqued. Making potions of any sort is my favourite thing to do! I carry my special

travelling potion kit with me wherever
I go, just in case, and if I can't take it with
me, I wear a secret necklace full of tiny
bottle charms filled with ingredients.
You never know when you might need
a potion!

'What sort of potion kit?' I asked.
'Is it the new updated *Witch-Twitch-Supreme*
I keep seeing on TV?'

'*Exactly* that one!' said Carlotta. 'Mum
and Dad said Edith needs it for her exams,
but it's so unfair!'

'Hmm,' I said, my mind filling with
the images from TV: a cauldron carved
from rose quartz crystal, a mixing spoon
hewn from amethyst, little bottles with

crystal toppers, and an unusual array of glittering ingredients I had never seen before.

'I'd love to see it!' I said, my fingers tingling. 'Just to *look* at it . . .'

'Oh, it's in Edith's room,' said Carlotta miserably. 'She'd never let us in.'

'We could go and knock and ask her *reeaally* nicely?' I suggested. 'Come on, Carlotta! I'd so love to see the *Witch-Twitch-Supreme* in real life!'

I hopped out of the hot tub and wrapped myself in a towel. Carlotta sighed and followed me out.

'You can ask.' Carlotta shrugged. 'But there's no way she'll say yes. She's so mean lately . . . Ever since she became a *teenager*, she thinks she's better than everyone else!'

Carlotta and I hurried back into the house dripping wet, leaving footprints along the floor. We ran up the stairs and banged on Edith's door. We had to bang very loudly because there was some spooky dance music coming from her bedroom. At last, the door flew open, and Edith stuck out her head. She looked like she had been dancing—her hair was all over the place! I had to bite my lip not to laugh.

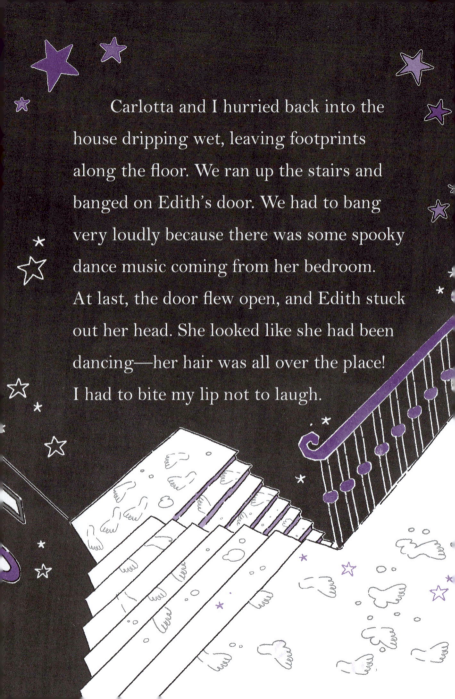

'What do you want, you little *froglets*?' she snapped.

I put on my sweetest and most innocent expression.

'We were just wondering, Edith,' I began, 'if you would show us your new potion kit? The one with the rose quartz cauldron and the amethyst spoon? I've never seen one like that before!'

Edith eyed us suspiciously.

'You two are *always* causing trouble,' she said. 'I don't trust you around my potion kit. You'd break it or something—and I don't have time. I have to get ready to go out.'

Then she slammed the door in our faces!

I turned to Carlotta in shock, my mouth agape.

'I told you,' said Carlotta, looking a little embarrassed. 'Edith's always in a mood these days . . .'

'*I heard that!*' Edith shouted from inside the room. The door flew open, and she stormed out and taped a piece of paper to it.

# KEEP OUT!!!

Then she marched back inside and slammed the door even louder!

Carlotta and I went across to her bedroom instead, and I started to unpack

the things from my suitcase, laying
out my favourite pair of frog-patterned
pyjamas that Mum and Dad had bought
me for the last time I went on a sleepover,
at Granny and Grandpa Starspell's house.

'I wonder where Edith is going
tonight,' I said.

'She's probably spending time with
her new *boyfriend*,' said Carlotta.

'Edith has a boyfriend?' I gasped.

Carlotta nodded. 'He goes to your
brother's wizard school!' she said.
'Wilbur might know him.'

'I'll have to ask . . .' I said. 'But *eww!*'

'*Eww!*' agreed Carlotta and we both
fell backwards laughing.

When we had recovered, we watched
Violet and Midnight—Carlotta's black
kitten—roll around imitating us on the floor.

Then we heard a door slam and a pair
of boots hurrying down the stairs. I got
up and peered out the window, Carlotta
following close behind.

We watched as Edith leapt onto her
broomstick and whooshed into the air,
looking *very* glamorous in a new black
cape shimmering with silver stars.

I turned to Carlotta.

'Edith's gone!' I said.

'Yes!' whispered Carlotta, a twinkle of
witchy mischief in her eyes. '*Shall we?*'

'There's no harm in *looking*,' I said.
'Just one tiny *look*?'

'Edith will *never know . . .*'

# Chapter TWO

Together we left Carlotta's room and tiptoed along the landing to Edith's. I felt prickles of excitement run up and down my spine as we stood in front of the *KEEP OUT* sign. It felt like Carlotta and I were on a secret mission. I knew it was a bit naughty to sneak into Edith's room without asking, but she had been so *mean* to us! And at least we weren't breaking any of Mr and Mrs Cobweb's rules. We weren't using *magic*.

Carlotta pushed the door open with a creak and we slipped inside.

KEEP OUT!!!

Edith's room was *enchanting*! It felt so much more grown-up than my room at home or Carlotta's. There was a big squishy chair in the corner covered in glittering green and purple stars, hundreds of crystal make-up and perfume bottles lined up on the dressing table, the bed was a *double* with swishy black velvet curtains, and on top of a bookcase stood the *Witch-Twitch-Supreme* potion kit!

'Oh!' I gasped, running over to it.

'Remember, we said *no touching the potion kit*,' said Carlotta, suddenly worried. 'It was very expensive.'

'I won't touch it,' I promised and clasped my hands behind my back. 'But *look*, Carlotta! It comes with a crystal ball!'

'I know . . .' sighed Carlotta enviously as we gazed at it together. My fingers were itching and tingling.

'It's so pretty,' I breathed. The rose
quartz cauldron glimmered and the
amethyst stirring spoon sparkled in the
light. I wished and wished and *wished* that
I was allowed to touch it!

Soon I felt too tempted to whip out my hand and stroke the crystal ball, so I turned away from the potion kit and moved over to the dressing table.

'Edith spends *sooo* long looking in the mirror nowadays,' said Carlotta. 'She's become a real bore! She never wants to play.'

'She's got a lot of spot creams,' I said, giggling.

My mum and dad own a beauty business, so I know all about make-up and skin creams, even though I'm not allowed to use any yet. They invent all kinds of magical perfumes and lipsticks and eyeshadows. Dad sources organic, environmentally friendly ingredients, and Mum brews the potions.

'I love that colour!' I said, pointing to a nail varnish stuffed towards the back of the dressing table. 'Acid green!'

'Me too,' said Carlotta, plucking out the bottle. 'Do you want me to paint your nails? Edith never wears it so she won't notice.'

'But we're not supposed to touch anything . . .'

'Well, we won't touch the *potion kit*,' said Carlotta, unscrewing the nail varnish.

A sharp smell filled the air. I sat down on the squishy chair, feeling a little more relaxed, stuck out my hand, and Carlotta

began to paint my nails. It wasn't just acid green, it came out black-and-green *stripy*!

'So cool!' I said, flapping my hands dry. 'Shall I do yours?'

Carlotta picked out
a bright red with black
ladybird spots, and after
I'd painted her nails, we
couldn't resist the rest of
Edith's make-up. We stuck
our fingers in the shimmery
eyeshadow and smudged it on
thickly. We dusted iridescent powder onto
our cheeks so that they glimmered and
glittered, and we spritzed ourselves with

perfumes that smelled
of marzipan
and purple
berries.

Then we poked through Edith's wardrobe, clomping around in her platform boots and trying on her spiderweb jewellery.

Eventually, I found myself back at the potion kit. When Carlotta wasn't looking, I stuck out my finger and gave the crystal ball a *teeny* little stroke. It felt *enchanting*. My fingertip fizzed with magic!

'*Oh no!*' I yelped.

'What is it?' asked Carlotta, looking round.

The crystal ball was GLOWING.

'Did you touch it?' asked Carlotta.

'Um . . . *maybe,*' I replied, my face flushing red. 'Will the glow fade?'

'I don't know.' Carlotta bit her lip, gazing around at the mess.

The carefree feeling turned to panic as I stared at Carlotta with her ladybird-spotted nails and eyes shimmering with witchy green glitter. I looked down at the

silvery spiderweb jewellery draped around my neck and at my nails which seemed to glow back at me in fierce acid stripes.

And then I looked at the GLOWING BALL.

*What had we been thinking?*

'Uh, Carlotta . . .' I said in a choked voice. 'I think we got carried away.'

'I think you're right.'

*'What are we going to do?'* I whispered.

'Tidy!' said Carlotta. 'Quickly! Before Edith gets home!'

She began to run around the room, picking things up and putting them away. I tried my best to help, but I couldn't remember where everything had come from, and the crystal ball wasn't fading *at all*. Suddenly, I had a burst of inspiration.

'Maybe it'll stop if I touch it again!' Before Carlotta could reply, I whisked the crystal ball off the shelf and held it up in the air.

It turned raspberry pink. 'Huh?'

Carlotta shrugged. 'I've heard they can be temperamental.'

I shook the crystal ball and the pink faded to sunset orange—then *blood red*. Desperate, I hurried over to the window and stuck my arms out, waving the ball around in the evening sunlight. It started to flash all the colours of the rainbow, smoke swirling within, and there came a faint ringing sound. Abruptly the fog cleared, and a *face* appeared!

'Hello?' it said.

'ARGHHH!' I shrieked.

And then I did the worst thing possible.

*I dropped the crystal ball.*

'NOOOO!' screamed Carlotta.


SMASH.

# Chapter THREE

Carlotta and I stared at each other in
horror as broken crystal tinkled on the
patio below.

'Oh my stars, oh my *stars*!' said
Carlotta, running over to the window.
'Did you forget that crystal balls can be
used as telephones, Mirabelle?'

'I thought you had to say a number

spell to call someone!' I wailed.

'No!' cried Carlotta. 'This is the *Witch-Twitch-Supreme*! You can have people on speed dial! That was my cousin Agnes! Oh, I hope she doesn't tell Edith . . .'

Carlotta looked close to tears, and I felt so incredibly guilty that I wished I could disappear in a puff of frog glitter.

'I'm *so* sorry, Carlotta. I didn't mean to drop it! When that face appeared, it just slipped out of my fingers! Maybe we can fix it . . . Have you got any glue? Edith might never notice!'

'She will notice!' said Carlotta. 'But maybe we *could* glue it back together, so

she might think she cracked it herself.
Come on, let's fetch the pieces.'

We ran downstairs and out into
the garden, where the crystal ball lay in
shards across the patio. Hurriedly, we
scooped them up into a wicker basket and
carried it into the house.

'Hello, girls!' said Mrs Cobweb as we passed her in the kitchen. 'What are you up to?'

'Umm,' said Carlotta, whipping the basket behind her back, 'we thought we'd do some gluing and sticking.'

'Crafting!' I squeaked.

We bolted out of the room and up the
stairs to Carlotta's bedroom, where she
tipped the shards onto the floor. We tried
our best to piece it back together.

'I *think* it looks OK,' said Carlotta as
she held the completed ball up to the light.
'Apart from all the cracks . . .'

'*Mmm*,' I hummed doubtfully.

'Well, there's nothing else to do,' said Carlotta. 'Let's just hope Edith doesn't notice!'

'Yes,' I agreed, my insides twisting with guilt. I knew deep down that what we were doing was wrong.

Downstairs, the front door banged open.

'Edith's back!' Carlotta hissed. 'I need to put it back in her bedroom!'

Carlotta disappeared and returned a few moments later looking flustered.

'Done!' she said, just as we began to hear Edith's boots climbing the stairs. We sat listening, as still and quiet as mice.

Edith reached the landing, walked past Carlotta's room, opened her own door, then closed it.

We waited, waited, waited for anything to happen.

*Surely Edith would notice!*

But there was nothing. Just . . . silence.

## 'DINNER TIME, WITCHES!'

We nearly jumped out of our *skin*!

'Ah, it's just Mum!' said Carlotta, relieved. 'Come on, let's try to forget about the crystal ball. It was only an accident, and she won't notice. Not tonight, anyway. Come on, we'd better wash our faces before dinner!'

'OK,' I said, my heart racing.

Down in the kitchen, we found Mrs Cobweb busy pouring different ingredients into bowls and a stack of pizza bases on the table.

'Pizza night!' she said. 'I thought it would be a nice treat, seeing as Mirabelle's staying over.'

'I love pizza!' cried Carlotta excitedly.

'Me too!' I said, trying to sound excited too. All I could think about was the crystal ball. I didn't *deserve* a treat.

Mrs Cobweb handed me a pizza base on a tray.

'You spread tomato sauce on it first,' she said, 'and then sprinkle on whichever toppings you like after. I've bought all sorts, including some special ones for you, Mirabelle. I heard that some fairies like *pineapple* pizza. Is that correct?'

'Yes,' I said. 'Thank you, Mrs Cobweb.'

I set to work spreading tomato sauce, sprinkling *loads* of cheese, and placing a few pieces of pineapple. *Yum*. Next to me, Carlotta covered her pizza with crispy beetles and lizard tails. *Yuck*. Witch food really is disgusting.

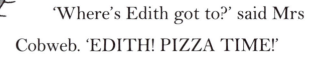

'Where's Edith got to?' said Mrs Cobweb. 'EDITH! PIZZA TIME!'

There came a clomping down the stairs and anxiety fluttered up inside me, but Edith just sauntered in with headphones on to assemble her own pizza. I relaxed a little.

When we had all finished, Mrs Cobweb slid the pizzas into the oven and laid the table. Edith did the washing up, and Carlotta and I did the drying.

'Edith always gets to do the washing!' complained Carlotta.

'That's because she's older, Carlotta,' said Mrs Cobweb. 'And you do rather *splash* everything.'

Eventually, our pizzas were ready, and we all sat down at the table to eat them, along with Mr Cobweb, who had just come in from work.

'I made your favourite kind,' Mrs Cobweb told him. '*Woodlouse!*'

'Delicious!' exclaimed Mr Cobweb. 'Thank you!'

I tried my best to eat my pineapple pizza—usually, it's my favourite—but my tummy felt all squiggly, and I kept glancing over at Edith and thinking about her broken crystal ball.

'Are you not hungry, Mirabelle?' asked Mrs Cobweb at the end of the meal. 'You've only eaten one slice!'

'I think I'm quite full from the delicious fairy cake earlier,' I said, not wanting to hurt Mrs Cobweb's feelings.

'Ah, never mind then!' said Mrs Cobweb with a smile. 'I'll put the rest in the fridge, and you can always eat it later.'

As soon as dinner was over, Carlotta
and I went back to her bedroom and got
into our pyjamas.

'What shall we do now?' asked
Carlotta. 'It's still a while until bedtime . . .
Ooh, let's watch a *horror film* and SCARE
ourselves to sleep!'

I agreed. Maybe the horror film would take my mind off Edith and the crystal ball. Carlotta and I dragged her duvet down the stairs and into the sitting room, then set up a cosy little nest for ourselves on the sofa.

'What shall we watch?' asked Carlotta. 'How about *The Curse of the Bog Witches*?'

'Maybe . . .' I said.

There was silence for a moment in the sitting room. All we could hear was the tick of the clock and then—

'*ARGHHHHH!*'

An ear-splitting scream came from above. An *Edith* scream.

I froze.

Carlotta froze.

'*CARLOTTAAAAA!*'

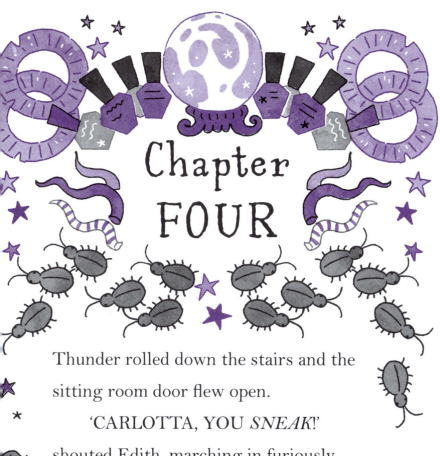

# Chapter FOUR

Thunder rolled down the stairs and the sitting room door flew open.

'CARLOTTA, YOU *SNEAK*!' shouted Edith, marching in furiously. 'You've been in my bedroom!'

'I haven't!' Carlotta squeaked.

'You HAVE!' screamed Edith. 'I can tell by the look on your face!'

'*I haven't,*' insisted Carlotta, but her cheeks had gone very red.

'You HAVE!' yelled Edith. 'You're a lying little WORM! I know you've been touching my stuff because *my crystal ball is broken*!'

She brought it out from behind her back and triumphantly held it in front of Carlotta's face. I felt my heart begin to race. It was *me* who broke the crystal ball! I should own up right that very second! But Edith looked so furious that I was too scared to open my mouth.

'*OK!*' said Carlotta. 'We *did* go in your room while you were out, but . . . But it was only so that we could *clean* it! I'm sorry the crystal ball broke. It fell off the shelf while I was dusting!'

I stared at Carlotta in shock. As if Edith was going to believe *that*!

Edith narrowed her eyes.

'YOU'RE A HORRIBLE MEDDLING SNEAKY SLIMY WORM, CARLOTTA!' she shrieked and stormed out of the room.

'Oh, Carlotta!' I said. 'Edith was never going to believe we went into her room to clean it!'

'I know,' said Carlotta, putting her

head in her hands. 'It was just the first thing that popped into my head . . . I didn't want to tell her the truth.'

'Oh!' I said, feeling a rush of affection for my friend just trying to protect me— but also a sharp stab of guilt. Now I felt even worse about not owning up.

'It's OK.' Carlotta shrugged. 'Edith and I are always arguing anyway, so she may as well think it was me!'

She smiled brightly, but it looked a bit forced.

'Let's find a horror film,' she said.

Carlotta and I sat side by side in the
dark, our eyes glued to the screen, but I
wasn't really watching the film. I couldn't
concentrate, and I didn't even jump at
the scariest parts! I felt such guilt about
the crystal ball. Carlotta had said it was

expensive! I should never have touched
it, and we should never have gone into
Edith's room in the first place! I would
*hate* it if Wilbur took his friends into *my*
room without asking and rooted around in
all my stuff!

'Shall we go to bed now?' asked Carlotta when the film came to an end.

I nodded. Neither of us mentioned the fact that we had agreed to stay up until midnight. I don't think we felt like having a midnight feast anymore.

I followed Carlotta up to her bedroom and laid my fairy cloud mattress and sleeping bag out on the floor. Then I went to the bathroom and brushed my teeth alone. This sleepover had stopped feeling fun. Usually, Carlotta and I spend ages in the bathroom messing around and poking about in all her mum's bath lotions and potions. But tonight, something felt . . . flat.

I returned to Carlotta's room and slipped inside my sleeping bag, hugging Violet tightly to my chest and feeling an unusual pang of homesickness. Everything just felt wrong.

'Goodnight, Mirabelle,' said Carlotta, turning out her bedside lamp. She didn't sound cross, but she didn't sound very happy either. Just a bit . . . deflated.

Usually, Carlotta and I tell ghost stories and stay up for hours giggling and chatting. Carlotta didn't seem to be in a chatty mood anymore. Maybe she was also feeling bad about sneaking into Edith's room? Maybe she felt responsible for the fact that her sister's precious crystal ball had got broken?

Or maybe she really *was* annoyed with me for not owning up?

That would be the worst . . .

'*Night, Carlotta,*' I whispered into
the darkness.

I tossed and turned on my mattress,
unable to get comfortable or sleep. I was
still awake when Mr and Mrs Cobweb
poked their heads around the door to say
goodnight, and I was still awake when
I heard them go to bed an hour later. I lay
there in the dark, listening to the tick-tock
of the clock on the wall and the steady
breathing of Carlotta, already asleep.
I felt like I had been lying there forever—
so long that my tummy was starting
to grumble.

I sat up in bed. It had been
*ages* since the pizza, and I had only
managed one slice. No wonder I was
so hungry! Maybe if I snuck down to
the kitchen and ate some more,
I might get to sleep.

I slipped out of bed, careful not
to wake Violet or disturb Carlotta.
I grabbed my fairy wand and lit it
like a torch, tiptoeing to the door
then out onto the landing and down
the stairs. Tiptoe, tiptoe, tiptoe . . .
The house felt different at night.
Creepier. Full of shadows. I shivered,
glad that I had brought my wand to
light the way.

I snuck to the kitchen and pushed the
door open, hoping that it wouldn't creak.
I peered inside and stopped in my tracks,
the breath catching in my throat.

There was a sinister, silhouetted figure sitting at the kitchen table!

A figure wearing pyjamas and cradling a mug of hot bogwater. The figure twisted round. I jumped.

'Oh, it's just you, Mirabelle!'

'*Edith?*'

# Chapter FIVE

I sidled over to the table, my fairy wand lighting up Edith's face. She looked a bit sad.

'What are you doing down here? I asked.

'To be honest . . .' said Edith. 'I was feeling *guilty.*'

'*You* were feeling *guilty*?' I said. 'I'm the one who should be feeling guilty, Edith.

*I broke your crystal ball!* I'm so, so sorry. It was a mistake. I only stroked it once and then it lit up and I didn't *mean* to drop it out of the window, but it started ringing and there was a *face*—'

My words were all coming out in a gabble. It all just sounded like excuses.

I stopped. Took a breath.

'I'm really sorry,' I said again.

'Carlotta and I shouldn't have been in your room, touching all your stuff. I'm going to save up my pocket money and buy you a new crystal ball, I promise.'

Edith smiled.

'Thank you, Mirabelle,' she said. 'I *knew* you two didn't go in my room to tidy it!'

She chuckled and I managed a smile.

'Why are *you* feeling bad?' I asked her.

'I shouldn't have shouted at Carlotta like that,' sighed Edith. 'It was mean. Or shut you both out of my room earlier. If I'd just let you in and shown you the potion kit in the first place, the crystal ball might never have got broken!'

That sounded true, but it still didn't make it OK for Carlotta and me to have snuck into Edith's room without asking.

'Carlotta and I are always *arguing* nowadays,' continued Edith. 'We used to play together all the time, but now . . . I find her games boring. And she doesn't understand that sometimes I want *privacy*!'

'My big brother Wilbur is the same,'

I said, nodding. 'He hardly ever plays the games I want to play. But you know what? I love joining in with his! Most of the time he doesn't mind *too much*. I bet Carlotta would love doing things *you* like. She loves painting her nails and all that stuff!'

Edith raised an eyebrow. 'I *did* notice your nails . . .'

Blushing, I hid my fingers under the table.

*Whoops!*

Edith took a sip of her hot bogwater, and my tummy grumbled loudly, even though I *hate* witchy drinks.

'Are you hungry?' asked Edith. 'Or thirsty? Do you want me to make you some bogwater?'

'Er . . . No, thank you,' I replied politely. 'I'm not a fan. It's a bit gritty for my fairy tastes.'

'I love it gritty!' said Edith, licking her lips. 'The *grittier* the better! What do fairies drink for a treat?'

'Hot chocolate!' I said. 'Or milkshake! Or ice cream fizz. Or raspberry crush!'

'Sounds disgusting . . .' replied Edith. 'I can't even imagine what those drinks look like.'

'I can show you!' I said, waving my wand so that a tall glass of pink milkshake with a swirl of raspberry cream and chocolate sprinkles appeared on the table.

My mouth watered looking at it. The best thing about being half fairy is having a wand to magic up whatever I like to eat! I don't do it all the time as Mum and Dad insist that we eat healthily most days. But I am allowed to magic up food on special occasions.

I took a sip of the milkshake.

'Do you want to try some?' I asked.

'Er . . . No, thank you,' replied Edith, equally politely. 'I think I'll stick to the hot bogwater. Hey! This is kind of like a *midnight feast*!'

'It is!' I agreed. 'Maybe we should wake Carlotta up? She'd be disappointed to miss it.'

'I think you're right,' nodded Edith. 'I'll make her a cup of hot bogwater, and we can carry some snacks up to my bedroom. We'll lay it all out nicely and then go and wake Carlotta up!'

'*Your* bedroom!?' I said, shocked.

'Sure.' Edith smiled. 'I'm *inviting* you this time.'

Ten minutes later, Edith and I tiptoed
back up the stairs, both holding trays full
of delicious food for our midnight feast.
I had found the rest of my pizza in the
fridge, and I couldn't wait to tuck
in. I was so hungry!

When we got to Edith's room, she laid a star-spangled rug out on the floor, and we arranged the food on it nicely. Edith had brought up the rest of the cupcakes and found some gummy worms at the back of a cupboard for her and Carlotta—and a big bag of salt and vinegar crispy spiders' legs!

'Let's go wake her up!' Edith whispered when we were ready.

Together, she and I hurried along the landing to Carlotta's room. I felt butterflies of excitement flutter in my tummy. This was going to be a *real* and *proper* midnight feast!

'Carlotta!' whispered Edith, shaking her sister gently. 'Carlotta, wake up!'

Carlotta stirred, then blearily opened her eyes, frowning in the light of my wand.

'Edith?' she said, confused. 'What's going on?'

Edith sat down on Carlotta's bed and gave her sister a big hug.

'I'm sorry I was mean to you earlier,'
she said. 'I should've been nicer when you
asked to come in. And I know it wasn't
you who broke the crystal ball.'

I hung my head, still a bit ashamed
that I had let Carlotta take the blame.

Carlotta rubbed her eyes sleepily.

'Oh, it's all right,' she yawned. 'I didn't want you to shout at Mirabelle, that was all. And I'm used to you being annoyed at me, so . . .'

Edith looked sad.

'I'm sorry I always seem annoyed with you,' she said. 'I *have* been more shouty than usual lately . . . And I'm sorry for always shutting you out of my bedroom.'

'I'm sorry we snuck into your bedroom without asking,' said Carlotta. 'We shouldn't have done it.'

'It's OK,' replied Edith. 'How about we all go there now? I'll show you my

potion kit properly and we can have a MIDNIGHT FEAST!'

'Your bedroom? Really!?' Carlotta cried, her face brightening as she swung her legs out of bed. 'And *ooh! A midnight feast!*'

'*Shh!*' hissed Edith. '*We don't want to wake Mum and Dad!*'

Together, the three of us snuck back across the landing to Edith's room and shut the door quietly. Carlotta took my hand and gave it a squeeze. We didn't need to say anything to each other, but I knew that everything was good again! My heart felt big and glowing. It made me really happy to see Edith and Carlotta smiling and laughing together.

Edith fetched her potion kit from the shelf and showed it to us properly. The rose quartz cauldron really was beautiful!

'Oof! It's heavy!' said Carlotta, trying to lift it.

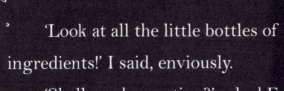

'Look at all the little bottles of
ingredients!' I said, enviously.

    'Shall we do a potion?' asked Edith,
her eyes twinkling.

'Mum and Dad said no magic tonight . . .' pointed out Carlotta.

'Oh, but they didn't tell *me* not to do any magic!' said Edith.

She poured a selection of ingredients into the cauldron and then stirred them up with the amethyst crystal spoon, murmuring some magic words. Carlotta and I leant forwards, intrigued to see what would happen. A beautiful, iridescent, rainbowy, glittery mixture swirled at the bottom of the cauldron.

'It's a new nail polish!' said Edith.

'Oh,' said Carlotta, looking down at her nails a little disappointedly. 'I wish I hadn't painted mine already. That colour is much prettier!'

'Well, you've still got *toenails*, haven't
you?' cackled Edith.

By the time we had finished all the food and painted each other's toenails (and Edith's fingernails) it was very, very late. Outside, the black sky twinkled all over with stars, and the three of us couldn't stop yawning. We crawled up onto Edith's big four-poster bed, pulled the curtains round it, and fell into a deep, contented sleep.

# Chapter SIX

Waking up the next morning, I was
surprised to find myself in Edith's bed, but
then the memories of our midnight feast
came flooding back. I stuck my foot into the
air and wiggled my toes, watching how the
iridescent nail polish glimmered and gleamed.

'Ah, you're awake!' said Carlotta,
sounding pleased.

'Don't wake me yet!' moaned Edith, pressing her pillow over her head and rolling over.

Carlotta and I slipped out of bed and hurried out of the room, leaving Edith to sleep a bit longer.

'You know,' said Carlotta as we went down the stairs, 'I don't really feel hungry for breakfast at all!'

'Breakfast?!' said Mr Cobweb as we arrived down in the kitchen. 'It's *lunchtime* now, girls! I'm just about to make it.'

Carlotta and I glanced at each other, sharing a secret look. It had been a *magical* night!

'Why don't you go and wake Edith?'
suggested Mrs Cobweb, who was busy
sweeping the floor. 'I know she
likes to sleep in at the weekends,
but really! This takes the bog-
biscuit!'

Carlotta turned and made
as though to walk back up the
stairs—but then she stopped.

'I think Edith needs
her *space* this morning,'
Carlotta said. 'I'm sure
she'll come down when
she's ready.'

Mrs Cobweb
looked surprised.

'Hmm. Maybe you're right,' she said after a moment. 'She is a teenager now after all. You two had better go and get dressed for . . . What *are* you planning to do today?'

'We were hoping to earn some money,' I said.

'Ooh yes!' said Carlotta. 'Have you got any odd jobs for us?'

'Money?' said Mrs Cobweb.

'Whatever for?'

I was about to make up an excuse, but then I remembered everything that had happened the night before. Things would have been made right *much* sooner if I had owned up straight away.

'I broke Edith's crystal ball, Mr and Mrs Cobweb,' I said in a rush. 'By mistake. And now I want to replace it.'

'It wasn't *just* Mirabelle's fault either,' added Carlotta, loyally.

'I see!' said Mrs Cobweb—but she didn't look cross. 'Thank you for being honest, Mirabelle. I'm sure it was an accident, and it's very sweet that you want to replace it. I wonder what jobs we could get you both to do . . .'

An excited look came over her face.

'My broomstick could do with a polish!' she said. 'And the bathroom needs scrubbing. So does the hot tub now that I think about it. And the nettles could do with cutting back in the garden. And you could make the lunch for everyone too.'

'I was about to make slug sandwiches!' added Mr Cobweb. 'But you can both take over.'

Carlotta and I gazed at each other in dismay. I don't think Mr or Mrs Cobweb noticed. They looked *delighted*!

'We'll go and put our feet up in the sitting room for a change,' said Mrs Cobweb. 'If you could just bring us a cup of hot bogwater in a few minutes, that would be wonderful. Thank you, girls!'

Then they both disappeared out of the room, humming.

'I guess we *kind of* deserve this,' said Carlotta.

'I'm sure we can make it fun,' I said, as a spark of witchy mischief glittered inside me. 'Your mum and dad didn't say anything about us using magic *today*, did they?'

'That's true!' said Carlotta. Her eyes began to twinkle impishly too. 'I'm sure there's a *potion* or two we could use . . .'

# Quiz

What kind of sleepover friend are you?
Take the quiz to find out!

### 1. What's your favourite thing to do at a sleepover?

**A.** Play fun games

**B.** Tell silly stories and try to make each other laugh

**C.** Have a cosy movie night with yummy snacks

### 2. What's your ideal sleepover snack?

**A.** Ice cream with rainbow sprinkles

**B.** Cheesy pizza

**C.** Hot chocolate with marshmallows

### 3. What's your ideal sleepover bedtime?

**A.** I want to stay up all night!

**B.** I'd stay up a little past bedtime, but not too late.

**C.** I'd go to bed at the normal time. I need my beauty sleep!

# Results

## Mostly As

You're an adventurous and fun-loving sleepover friend! You enjoy exciting activities and games, making every sleepover unforgettable.

## Mostly Bs

You're the life of the sleepover party! Your silly and humorous nature brings joy to everyone, and your storytelling skills are unbeatable.

## Mostly Cs

You're the cosy and caring friend at the sleepover! You love relaxing activities like movie nights and enjoy making sure everyone is comfortable and happy.

To visit Harriet Muncaster's
website, visit
harrietmuncaster.co.uk

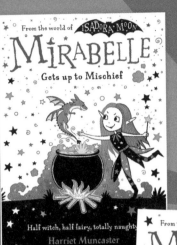

From the world of ISADORA MOON

# MIRABELLE
## Gets up to Mischief

Half witch, half fairy, totally naughty!
Harriet Muncaster

From the world of ISADORA MOON

# MIRABELLE
## Has a Bad Day

From the world of ISADORA MOON

# MIRABELLE
## Breaks the Rules

Half witch, half fairy, tot...
Harriet Munc...

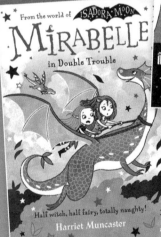

From the world of ISADORA MOON

# MIRABELLE
## in Double Trouble

Half witch, half fairy, totally naughty!
Harriet Muncaster

From the world of ISADORA MOON

# MIRABELLE
## and the Naughty Bat Kittens

Half witch, half fairy, totally naughty!
Harriet Muncaster

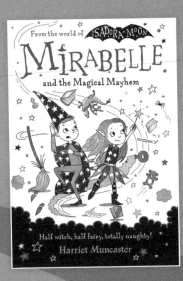

From the world of ISADORA MOON

# Mirabelle

### and the Magical Mayhem

Half witch, half fairy, totally naughty!

Harriet Muncaster

From the world of ISADORA MOON

# MIRABELLE

### Takes Charge

Half witch, half fairy, totally naughty!

Harriet Muncaster

From the world of ISADORA MOON

# MIRABELLE

### Wants to Win

Half witch, half fairy, totally naughty!

Harriet Muncaster

From the world of ISADORA MOON

# MIRABELLE

### and the Haunted House

Half witch, half fairy, totally naughty!

Harriet Muncaster

# ISADORA MOON

ISADORA MOON
Goes to School
Half vampire, half fairy, totally unique!
Harriet Muncaster

ISADORA MOON
Goes Camping
Half vampire, half fairy, totally unique!
Harriet Muncaster

ISADORA MOON
Has a Birthday
Half vampire, half fairy, totally unique!
Harriet Muncaster

ISADORA MOON
Goes to the Ballet
Half vampire, half fairy, totally unique!
Harriet Muncaster

ISADORA MOON
Gets in Trouble
Half vampire, half fairy, totally unique!
Harriet Muncaster

ISADORA MOON
Goes on a School Trip
Half vampire, half fairy, totally unique!
Harriet Muncaster

ISADORA MOON
Goes to the Fair
Half vampire, half fairy, totally unique!
Harriet Muncaster

ISADORA MOON
Makes Winter Magic
Half vampire, half fairy, totally unique!
Harriet Muncaster

ISADORA MOON
Has a Sleepover
Half vampire, half fairy, totally unique!
Harriet Muncaster

*ISADORA MOON*
Puts on a Show
Half vampire, half fairy, totally unique!
Harriet Muncaster

*ISADORA MOON*
Goes on Holiday
Half vampire, half fairy, totally unique!
Harriet Muncaster

*ISADORA MOON*
Goes to a Wedding
Half vampire, half fairy, totally unique!
Harriet Muncaster

*ISADORA MOON*
Meets the Tooth Fairy
Half vampire, half fairy, totally unique!
Harriet Muncaster

*ISADORA MOON*
and the Shooting Star
Half vampire, half fairy, totally unique!
Harriet Muncaster

*ISADORA MOON*
Gets the Magic Pox
Half vampire, half fairy, totally unique!
Harriet Muncaster

*ISADORA MOON*
Under the Sea
Half vampire, half fairy, totally unique!
Harriet Muncaster

*ISADORA MOON*
and the New Girl
Half vampire, half fairy, totally unique!
Harriet Muncaster

*ISADORA MOON*
and the Frost Festival
Half vampire, half fairy, totally unique!
Harriet Muncaster

Get ready to meet
Isadora's mermaid
friend, Emerald!

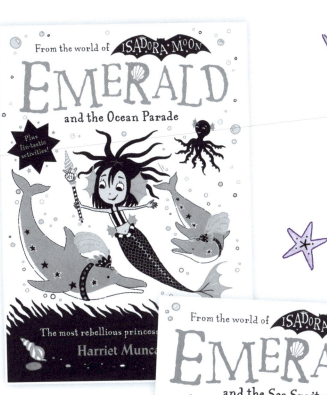

From the world of ISADORA MOON

# EMERALD
### and the Ocean Parade

Plus fin-tastic activities!

The most rebellious princess

Harriet Munc

From the world of ISADORA MOON

# EMERALD
### and the Sea Sprites

The most rebellious princess under the sea

Harriet Muncaster

# Harriet Muncaster

Harriet Muncaster, that's me! I'm the creator
of three young fiction series, Isadora Moon,
Mirabelle, and Emerald, as well as the
Victoria Stitch series for older readers.
I love anything teeny tiny, anything starry,
and everything glittery.

# Love Mirabelle?
# Why not try these too...